The Dawdlewalk

The Dawdlewalk

by Tobi Tobias

Carolrhoda Books
Minneapolis

pictures by
Jeanette Swofford

The illustrations for this book were prepared in charcoal pencil and watercolor
and printed on Starwhite-Vicksburg Natural Text.
The text type is Century Old Style. The display type is Bold and Light neo-Montauk.
Color separations and printing by Spectrum, Inc., Minneapolis
Typesetting by P & H Photo Composition, Minneapolis
Bound by Muscle Bound Bindery, Inc., Minneapolis
Design by Gale Houdek

Manufactured in the United States of America

Library of Congress Cataloging in Publication Data
Tobias, Tobi.
The dawdlewalk.
Summary: Both mother and youngster
discover there is so much to see on the way
to school that dawdling is inevitable.
[1. Mother and child—Fiction. 2. School
stories] I. Swofford, Jeanette, ill. II. Title.
PZ7.T56Daw   [E]   81-21666
ISBN 0-87614-190-4   AACR2

1 2 3 4 5 6 7 8 9 10 90 89 88 87 86 85 84 83

for Lucyle Hook

Every morning you and your mother walk to school. You walk and you walk and . . .

You stop to watch some sparrows having breakfast. Somebody's given them a crust of bread and they scoot around it, pecking and flapping their wings. And one takes a drink from last night's rain puddle. First he takes a sip and then he tips his head so the water can trickle down. Sip, tip, sip, tip—

And your mother says, "Come on, dear, no dawdling now. You want to get to school on time."

So you walk and you walk and . . .

You stop to look into the supermarket window. It's all filled with wonderful boxes of crunchy cereal like Rocket Crisps and Nature's Best and Mr. Sweet-O that you saw on t.v. and Prize o' Plenty that has that thing on the back you can send away and get a toy—

And your mother says, "Come on, dear, if we hurry we can just make this light." So you walk and you walk and . . .

You stop in front of the bakery where the fat black-and-white cat lives. She has a red collar with sparkly green stones on it. Is she there this morning? Yes, there she is, in that patch of sun, licking herself clean. She's rubbing her paw over her face, and then suddenly she stops and looks straight up at you—

And your mother says, "Come on, dear, if we stop for every single cat we see, we'll never get there at all."

So you walk and you walk and . . .

You stop to watch the sweeper truck coming up the street. It squirts out some water and its big fat brushes go 'round and 'round, and all the dirt gets swooshed away—

840499

And your mother says, "Come on, dear, you've seen it a hundred times, it'll be here again tomorrow."

So you walk and you walk and . . .

You stop because you see the man with the white hair. He's always sitting in a chair in front of Mr. Fields' hardware store, leaning on his cane. And he always says "How's the boy?" or "How's the girl?" when a kid passes by. When you were littler you used to be a little afraid of him. But now you go over and say, "I'm fine, how are you?" and "Did you see my friend go by yet, the one with the funny red hat—"

And your mother says, "Come on, dear, say good-bye now, we really must get going." So you walk and you walk and . . .

Right across the street from school your mother meets a friend and they start talking, oh, about news in the world and people they know and things like that. And they stand there talking and laughing and talking some more.

But you see all your friends, and you remember that your class is starting a new project today, and you think you hear the bell going to ring . . .

... and you pull your mother's hand and say, "Come on, Mommy. I'm in a hurry."